GRIT & Bear It!

Written by **Tamara Zentic**, M.S.

Illustrated by **Lisa M. Griffin**

BOYS TOWN Press

Boys Town, Nebraska

To my three children: Lindsey, *Kaitlin* & **Zane**,
Never be afraid to get your hands **"EXTRA"** dirty!
I believe **"YOU CAN!"** always!

GRIT & Bear It!
Text and Illustrations
Copyright © 2014 by Father Flanagan's Boys' Home
978-1-934490-64-8

Published by the Boys Town Press
14100 Crawford St., Boys Town, NE 68010

**For a Boys Town Press catalog,
call 1-800-282-6657 or visit
BoysTownPress.org**

Boys Town Press is the publishing
division of Boys Town, a national
organization serving children
and families.

Publisher's Cataloging-in-Publication Data

Zentic, Tamara.
Grit & bear it! / written by Tamara Zentic, MS ; illustrated by Lisa M. Griffin. -- Boys Town, NE : Boys Town
Press, [2014]

p. ; cm.
(From black & white to living color)
ISBN: 978-1-934490-64-8
Audience: grades 5-10.
Summary: Through illustrations and straight-forward statements, middle school children are introduced to
"grit"-- a combination of self-determination and a willingness to take risks and bounce back from failure. This
is the first book in the "From black & white to living color" series.--Publisher.

1. Middle school students--Life skills guides. 2. Teenagers--Life skills guides. 3. Autonomy in adolescence.
4. Self-reliance in adolescence. 5. Risk-taking (Psychology) in adolescence. 6. Failure (Psychology) in adolescence. 7. Judgment in adolescence. 8. Adolescent psychology. 9. [Conduct of life. 10. Self-reliance. 11. Risk tak-
ing (Psychology) 12. Failure (Psychology) 13. Judgment.] I. Griffin, Lisa M. (Lisa Middleton), 1972- II. Title.
BF724.3.A88 Z46 2014
155.5/1346--dc23   1408

Printed in the United States
10 9 8 7 6 5 4 3 2 1

A *small* but MIGHTY WORD

You may not know who **I am...**

You may not know
my meaning...

Maybe you have never
spoken my name...

4

Once you know it...

You may turn and
run from me

5

Trying **hard**
to *push me away*

Hoping that somehow you
will never need to use me

7

Instead, you might try to
take the *easy way out*

8

Where *gratification* is **instant**
And all things are given easily

Because I will take the
most from you,

day
after
day

For **I am**

HARD

to

OBTAIN

My road is the difficult one

Requiring

RelEnTLesS

effort

I

demand

you roll up your sleeves and

get dirty

Giving me your sweat,
tears, and all that you have

With **me,** time knows **no bounds**

I consume

those who embrace me...
Those who strive to be better...

$$\frac{x^2-4}{x+3}$$

$$xy = \frac{v^2}{2v^2}y^4$$

to be
accomplished
to be
successful...

I am
free

Yet, you **must pay** the price

$\mathcal{I}$ may seem like a

long
shot...

But you will relish the payoff

I overcome **trials,**

23

setbacks,

and **failures**...

I give confidence, **determination,** and **satisfaction...**

26

Through me
you can hold
your head high

I form

character

I am able to
make you more than you have
ever **imagined**

I can lead you to the

Most *and the* Best

that you can be

I am

GRIT!

Generating • Relentless • Inner • Toughness

A Note to Parents and Educators

$$E = mc^2$$

$$f(x) = a$$

Having GRIT has become an important issue for youth today.

Some people consider **GRIT** to be the biggest indicator of future success in all areas of life. **GRIT** – the ability and drive to work hard, persevere through trials and failures, and overcome hardships – is a foundational block upon which many of life's success stories are built. Many individuals start out on the path to great success and achievement, yet few have the necessary **GRIT** to stay the course as they pursue their goals and dreams.

Here are a few tips for helping children develop more GRIT:

- Start when children are young – Remember that it's never too late to develop **GRIT.**
- Instill a growth mindset – Children need to believe that through hard work, they can grow past their current level of performance.
- Have reasonable expectations – Children may not reach their goals the first time, or every time.
- Applaud effort as well as the end result.
- Teach children how to delay gratification.
- Set a good example and work together – Your own work ethic speaks volumes to children about your own **GRIT!**
- Help children see their mistakes and failures as opportunities for progress.
- Teach children to use positive self-talk.
- Encourage children to build life-long positive habits – Encourage them to be intentional about setting good habits and goals throughout life. Remember, they don't have to do it all at once.
- Hold children accountable for demonstrating **GRIT**-developing behaviors and actions.
- Teach children how to rethink problems – Remind them that frustrations, setbacks, and a lack of enthusiasm are common, and show them how to avoid giving up.
- Use the **A.R.M. Technique (Raising your arm in triumph!): Assess** the problem; **Re-evaluate/Rethink** the next step; **Move on!**

Life gets hard! By nature and through life events, some people possess or develop more **GRIT** than others. But that shouldn't deter us. *Anyone,* at any age, through a few simple strategies, can develop more **GRIT (Generating Relentless Inner Toughness)!**

For more parenting information, visit parenting.org

from **BOYS TOWN**

Boys Town Press
Featured Titles

978-1-934490-59-4

978-1-934490-64-8

978-1-934490-65-5

Look for the next title in the
From Black & White to Living Color series: ***ZEST!***